THE LITTLE ASPEN BOY

KATIE CLARKE HEAD

authorHOUSE®

AuthorHouse™
1663 Liberty Drive
Bloomington, IN 47403
www.authorhouse.com
Phone: 1 (800) 839-8640

Published by AuthorHouse 04/19/2017

ISBN: 978-1-5246-8647-5 (sc)
ISBN: 978-1-5246-8646-8 (e)

Library of Congress Control Number: 2017905216

Print information available on the last page.

Any people depicted in stock imagery provided by Thinkstock are models, and such images are being used for illustrative purposes only. Certain stock imagery © Thinkstock.

This book is printed on acid-free paper.

DEDICATION

I am beyond thrilled to dedicate my very first Children's Fable to my precious Nieces and Nephews, who are my biggest loves and inspirations; Emma (The Exquisite & Kind Hearted Bunny), Tessa (The Delightful & Exotic Doe), Lyla (The Adorable and Spirited Kitten), Tyler (The Protective & Glorious Mountain Black Bear), Timmy (The Special Little Aspen Boy), Matthew (The Brilliant & Energetic Blue Bird) and Christian (The Playful and Courageous Berenice Mountain Dog).

You have all filled my heart with tremendous joy and your pure beauty, wisdom, kindness, love and laughter have brightened my life. I am so honored and proud to know and love each of you!

My greatest wish for my Little Ones is for you to always and forever follow your dreams, spread your wings grandly and soar to your greatest desires.

All My Love,
Aunt KT

SPECIAL THANKS

This beautiful Story was a true Labor of Love. There were so many times throughout the years when I truly thought this amazing Dream would never be completed, let alone Published.

Every time I lost my way and set my pen and pad aside, miraculously, my Guardian Angel would reappear with all of her unwavering encouragement, cheering, loyalty, determination and true belief in me!

She helped me to spread my wings & soar to my greatest heights! With sincere and special thanks, I also dedicate this Book to my brilliant and ever so talented…and cherished friend, Maureen "Moe" Eustis.

PART ONE

O nce upon a time in the quaint village of Old Antibes, in the South of France, lived a woman named Sophia and her husband Oliver. Sophia, a beautiful blonde-haired woman who was tall and elegant like a prima ballerina and Oliver, a tall and handsome gentleman with jet black hair and piercing blue eyes, lived a magical life and were deeply in love with each other. They delighted in spending all of their time together; relaxing in their charming estate located on the clear blue waters of the Mediterranean where they enjoyed dining on their patio, swimming and sailing. They owned a world-renown art and antiques gallery which was often patronized by artists, collectors, and famous people from near and far.

To everyone who was blessed to know them, they appeared to have the perfect life. But only Oliver and Sophia were aware of the deep sadness they shared about the one precious gift that was missing; the miracle of a child of their very own to love and cherish. After ten years of marriage, Sophia and Oliver still waited for the blessing of a baby. Sophia became heartbroken and began to lose hope of ever being able to share her heart with a child.

Oliver, who adored Sophia, was always comforting and optimistic, but deep down he was afraid of losing Sophia to her deep sadness. He stood by her side; gently and constantly urging her to start painting again. Painting had once brought her such joy and contentment when they first met. He also encouraged her to socialize more with her friends and the high society of the French culture, to which they had become accustomed.

Eventually, when nothing else seemed to ease her pain, Sophia took Oliver's advice and indulged in her amazing artistic talents. She slowly began to pour her sorrows into the exquisite masterpieces that she created and which Oliver then proudly hung in their home gallery. But she also secretly painted many nursery rhyme scenes in the hopes of one day hanging them in their child's nursery.

They gradually began to reenter the elegant social scene they once enjoyed, including galas, auctions and theatre openings. As one of the most popular socialite couples in all of France, they were encouraged and expected to attend these functions.

But as time passed by, try as they did to fill the void they shared from not being granted the gift of a child, they were unsuccessful. Soon enough they retreated back to their quiet solitary life in Antibes, where they settled for the peacefulness of their lovely home and the success of their gallery.

Then a miracle happened!

One morning, as Sophia sat on the porch enjoying a cup of tea, a croissant, and the breathtaking views of the matching cobalt blue sky and water, she felt suddenly ill. She knew instantly what was happening. Before sharing her suspicions with Oliver and getting his hopes up, she called Dr. Pierre Eustis and scheduled an appointment for that very morning. Dr. Eustis ran some tests and the results confirmed what Sophia was long hoping for!

That evening, over a romantic moonlit dinner, Oliver turned to Sophia and simply asked, "What is different about you this evening?" After all, she was glowing from head to toe and seemed to emit some emotion he couldn't quite put his finger on. Sophia asked Oliver to pick up his champagne glass for a toast. As he did, he caught a glimpse of a new ring she was wearing. It displayed the family's crest and there were baby booties engraved on it. As he met her eyes with confusion in his own, Sophia made a toast to Oliver congratulating him on being the proud father of their first born child. Their dreams had finally come true. Oliver's smile lit up the countryside as he sprang to his feet and scooped his wife up into his twirling embrace. Sophia laughed out loud at her husband's excitement.

As the months quickly passed, Sophia continued to glow and blossom. Pregnancy certainly suited her, just as preparing for fatherhood suited Oliver. He ran about creating a magical nursery for their unborn baby and happily waited on his precious wife, hand and foot, while always beaming from ear to ear.

The miraculous day finally came when precious little Timmy was born. He arrived with a healthy exclamation, rosy cheeks, and the most magnificent blue eyes anyone had ever seen. When he looked up at his parents for the very first time, a small smile appeared on his cherubic face. As it did, tears of joy rolled down the faces of Oliver and Sophia. They were finally a family!

Timmy's days were filled with joy, laughter and deep love. Sophia and Oliver would take their daily walks with Timmy and would proudly show him off to all of their friends in the village. Every person who came into contact with them was touched with the feeling of being in the presence of a special family.

One afternoon, when Timmy was almost two, Oliver came home from work late to find Sophia out back in the grass under a beautiful oak tree with Timmy nestled in her arms. They were both fast asleep. Silently, so as not to disturb this peaceful moment, he quickly went inside and grabbed his camera. Back outside he took one picture after another of Sophia and Timmy. To Oliver, these were not simple photographs; they were mental snapshots that would last a lifetime. And in that precious moment, he made a decision. He quietly walked over to his wife and son and knelt down

beside them. He then slipped a beautiful necklace with a pendant of the family crest and baby booties around her neck and gently fastened a matching charm bracelet on Timmy's tiny wrist. The baby booty charms on Timmy's bracelet were engraved with Sophia's name on one and Oliver's name on the other. Moments later Sophia began to stir from her reverie. Oliver took her hand in his and whispered that he was the luckiest man in the entire world. He also announced with great pride that he had planned a surprise family vacation for the three of them so they could continue to create memories that would last a lifetime.

One month later, Oliver, Sophia and Timmy landed at the Little Pitkin County Airport in Aspen, Colorado; home of the notoriously rich and famous. Aspen was not only quaint and glamorous; it also provided breathtaking views of the Rocky Mountains. After checking into a charming boutique hotel at the base of Aspen Mountain called The Little Haven, the trio spent the next few days sightseeing, shopping in the chic stores, strolling through the unique galleries, dining in the cozy bakeries and photographing everything they saw. As their vacation was nearing its end, they realized that the one thing they had not yet done, but truly wanted to do, was ski the majestic Rocky Mountains.

So the very next day, their last full day in Aspen, they arranged to meet their own personal ski valet, William, at The Little Haven. He fitted Sophie and Oliver with their state-of-the-art ski gear from head to toe and provided a sturdy white backpack for Timmy to ride in. Once they were finally outfitted, Matt accompanied them by foot to the base of Aspen Mountain, known to the locals as "Ajax" Mountain. There they would board one of the gondolas: the small enclosed cars which are pulled up the mountain on an overhead cable. He handed them their tickets and a very detailed trail map of the mountain, which Oliver tucked inside his ski jacket. After wishing them a great day full of fun runs, he cautioned them about a winter storm warning which had just been announced. The National Weather Service warned of the potential for blizzard conditions beginning later that evening. A concerned Oliver questioned William about whether they should cancel their trip. But William assured them that, if they followed the main trail on the map and were sure to be off the mountain by 3 o'clock p.m., they would be just fine. Because it was the last day of their vacation and they were all dressed and ready to go, they were reluctant to cancel their adventure. So, keeping in mind William's advice, they decided to enter the gondola.

Oliver and Sophia were very excited as they boarded the round pod that would deposit them at the top of the mountain. This was certainly a new adventure and Timmy squealed with laughter as the gondola began its mighty ascent and the town of Aspen became smaller by the second behind them. As the couple sat in the close quarters of the gondola holding hands and taking in the grandeur of the Rocky Mountains all around them, they realized once again how truly blessed they were. Simply put, their lives were complete. As Timmy, securely fastened in his backpack, peered over his father's shoulder, Sophia enjoyed the look of contentment on his sweet face.

After their scenic 18 minute ride to the very top of Aspen Mountain, they stepped off the gondola into another world. The view was panoramic and lovely. It took them a few moments to take in the 360 degrees of grandeur and activity.

There were crowds of people everywhere dressed in their finest ski attire, from mirrored goggles and designer sunglasses to helmets, ski pants, parkas, and the trendy one piece ski suits. Everyone's faces were dotted with rosy cheeks, responding to the fresh coolness of the mountain air. The sounds of fun and laughter rippled through the mountaintop and infected the young family of three as they watched skiers preparing for their descents and those simply enjoying a lazy afternoon dining on the outdoor patio of the famous Summit Restaurant with its spectacular postcard view of the Rockies. Taking it all in, Oliver was suddenly struck by the photographic opportunity presented by these scenes around him. It was important to him to always remember this exceptional experience, so he had brought

along his camera; hoping to add more photos to their personal family album, but also to one day include them in their art gallery back in the South of France. They had definitely made the right decision to ski Aspen Mountain, he thought. This experience was not to be missed!

Swiftly Oliver pulled out his camera and began shooting photo after photo as Sophia gently took Timmy out of his backpack so she could share with him this exciting experience: the vivid views, the pure whiteness of the snow, the magnificent height of the mountains, the luster of the trees, the warmth of the sun, the lively faces, and, most importantly, the inviting sound of laughter.

Oliver's attention was drawn to his stunning wife who was dressed in a white ski suit with a bright red hat and matching scarf, which mimicked the rosy glow of her cold cheeks. She was cuddling little Timmy snugly in her arms and gently swaying with him back and forth. As she talked to him, she spun him slowly around and around, as if they were dancing, to show him the spectacular view. Oliver was overcome with great pride and love for his family. He started taking one photo after another of them, not only with his camera, but with his heart and mind. A kind passerby, also taken by the sight of the beautiful woman and child, approached Oliver and said, "Would you like me to take a picture of you and your family together?" *Your* family. His family. Those words were magic to Oliver's ears and he gladly accepted the stranger's offer with a smiling "Merci". As he joined in the photo with Sophia and Timmy, Oliver already knew this would forever be his favorite family portrait.

Timmy began to get excited with the promise of the day and giggled as Sophia returned him to the backpack already strapped to Oliver's shoulders. Moments later they gently pushed off to take their very first fun down Aspen Mountain. They started off slowly on the intermediate and blue ski trails and began to acclimate themselves to the mountain. As they acquired their rhythm, their bodies started to remember the hundreds of ski trails they had traversed over the years and continents, and soon it was like they had just been on the slopes the day before.

What a wonderful time they all shared together. Up and down the mountain they went as the hours passed quickly by. Back on the mountaintop once again, they enjoyed pastries and hot chocolate on the patio of the Summit Restaurant. Little Timmy sat in the high chair wearing as much of the cookies and hot cocoa as he was consuming. This made his parents smile. They had all been famished from the exercise and Timmy made no secret of that fact. The mountain had been challenging, as expected, and they were beginning to feel it in their bodies. It was soon decided that they had only one more run left in them. After that, they would head back to the cozy hotel for a much deserved nap.

As they gathered their belongings, Oliver became vaguely aware of the disappearing sun. It seemed that the view wasn't as expansive as it had been, and the snow's glare wasn't as hard on his eyes as it once seemed. He paused to look around at the 360° view and the feeling of contentment he had been enjoying all day began to shift somewhat. He shook off the feeling and moved closer to his wife as she deposited their son into the backpack for the last time that day.

With their skis on, they approached the now familiar, and most popular, trail down Aspen Mountain—the main trail. Sophia knew it would be their last run and wondered if they'd ever be lucky enough to come back to this resort town again someday. With this in mind she said, "Mon cher, we have already taken this trail several times today. Why don't we try another one? We could even do the Black Diamond one over there." She pointed west. Oliver started to object, but it took only one more "S'il vous plait?" from Sophia and the decision was made. He loved to please his wife and, to be honest, he, too, was excited by the challenge of a difficult trail. They headed off to the far west side of Ajax where an arrow indicated (and warned of) a Black Diamond trail. As they started their long descent, they basked in the feeling of the deep powder and smiled broadly as they navigated the many moguls, one after the other.

Not long after they started down, a light snow began to fall and the brilliant blue sky that had framed their family photo only ten minutes earlier was now nowhere to be seen. It was then that Oliver remembered William's warning about the storm and about staying on the main trail. Certainly it wasn't 3 o'clock already. They had only just an hour ago seen a sun that was so high in the sky. Then again, when you are on a mountaintop two miles in the sky, the height of the sun can be deceiving, he thought to himself. He and his wife came to a stop together in time to witness the suddenly sunless sky. There was a new chill in the air that they hadn't felt before. It was at this moment they both realized that the falling snow had turned from a twinkling vision to a white-out cascade. What they were witnessing was not just a simple flurry. It was the beginning of the huge snowstorm William had warned them about.

Oliver skied over to the edge of the very narrow trail and Sophia quickly followed suit. In an effort to get his bearings, he removed his foggy goggles and let them settle around his neck. With the heavy snowfall it was impossible to see. He was becoming disoriented. They needed to get back to the main trail with everyone else. Where exactly were they on this massive mountain? Removing his gloves, he tried to pull out the trail map from his inside jacket pocket, but the straps of Timmy's backpack prevented him from unzipping his coat. Sophia struggled a bit to help

Oliver unclip the pack and then she lifted it, with Timmy bundled tightly inside, off of her husband's back. The pack seemed heavier than it was earlier that day. The late hour-and trepidation-was making her tired. She sat the pack upright on the ground and couldn't help but marvel at her son, wrapped tightly in his blanket, sleeping as if he hadn't a worry in the world. Fortunately he was unaware of the dread which was quickly consuming his parents. Knowing that Timmy was cozy and safe on the edge of the trail, Sophia moved over to Oliver's side and tried to read the trail map over his broad shoulder. It was hard to know where they should go when they didn't even know where they were.

They knew the storm would have created a mass exodus of skiers down the mountain. The problem was that the trio chose an unpopular trail for their final fun; and an unpopular mode for that matter. Most of the other skiers would be taking the safest and surest way down: the gondolas. This meant the family was unlikely to encounter fellow skiers with whom they could band together for safety.

"Mon Dieu." Sophia's nearly inaudible whisper let Oliver know that she was deeply worried and now feared for their lives, especially Timmy's. The snowfall became impossibly thick and the quickening winds let them know that they needed to act swiftly to get to safety. Oliver firmly grabbed Sophia by her arms and spoke directly into her wide eyes.

He said, "Sophie, darling, everything is going to be okay. I would never let anything happen to you and Timmy. We will continue the way we were going and arrive in Aspen before you know it." Sophia held back the big tears that were forming and hugged Oliver. She relaxed slightly with his reassurances. They broke the embrace together, strengthened in their resolve to get moving down the mountain. Oliver replaced his goggles on his face as Sophia turned toward Timmy in his backpack.

The scream that came from Sophia's mouth was horrific and quickly absorbed by the thick curtain of falling snow. To the average person's ears it was not a sound any human could have made. It was primal and animalistic.

Little Timmy was gone. He had simply disappeared.

Oliver looked stricken as he grabbed her by the shoulders to ask her what was so suddenly wrong. She pushed off Oliver with both of her hands and rushed over to the exact spot where she had put her sleeping toddler only minutes before. Or at least to the spot she *thought* she had put him. "Timmy!!" she screamed. To her horror she realized that the snow had already covered the tracks she had made with her boots when she had walked to Oliver's side. She turned around and around but it was useless. Her husband was instantly beside her. They dropped to their knees at the same time and began sweeping their arms across the snow in a frantic effort to uncover their son. They crawled around hollering out his name and poking the drifts along the trail's edge with their ski poles. Abruptly they stopped at the same time to listen for their son's cries but the only sounds they could hear were the howling wind and their own erratic breathing.

Minutes passed by. Oliver grasped Sophia's hand and calmly told her that their only chance to find their Timmy in this horrific blizzard was to go for help. They had to find the ski patrol. But they couldn't go up so they had no choice but to go down. If that failed, they had to somehow reach the bottom of the mountain and tell the search and rescue team that their son was missing.

Sophia urged Oliver to go for help, but wanted no part in leaving her son alone. She was adamant that she was staying exactly where she was to keep looking for little Timmy. Oliver begged her to come with him, for he could not imagine leaving her, too, and feared that she may freeze to death in the high altitude temperatures and biting wind. But Sophia was insistent and would not budge. Her maternal instincts told her she could not leave Timmy again.

Finally, left with no other choice, Oliver hugged Sophia tightly and told her that he loved her deeply. He made her promise to stay exactly where she was until he returned with help, which he assured her he would. He placed his goggles and gloves back on, put his hands through the straps on his ski poles and quickly pushed off in the direction he thought the main ski trail was. As an afterthought, he stopped

at a nearby Aspen tree and broke some branches off its towering frame. He hoped to use them to mark the path back to his family.

As Oliver skied east he continued to drop branch after branch in his wake. After several minutes he realized that he could not see even his hand in front of his face, nor could he make out any light coming from the town at the base of the mountain. He couldn't even hear any voices of the fellow skiers who most certainly must be trying to get down the mountain as well. Although he tried to avoid the reality that over an hour had passed since they departed on their last run, Oliver had to acknowledge that it was getting later and later and, like the mountain sky, his thoughts were turning dark. Certainly, he thought, all of the day skiers were safe and sound at the bottom of the mountain by now; already recounting the story of their blizzard adventure over freshly poured glasses of wine. The ski patrol had most likely finished their last safety route for the day and was putting their ski mobiles to rest for the night.

Oliver knew that the only way to get the help they needed was to ski all the way to the bottom of the mountain where he would find the ski patrol office. But he rejected the idea of leaving this mountain without his family and headed back in the direction of Sophia and Timmy. With amazement he realized that the only indication of where he had come from was the branches he himself had stuck upright in the snow. His ski tracks had already been buried by a smooth layer of snow. Exhausted, he eventually reached the spot where he had left Sophia. He hoped in vein that she had managed to find their son and the two were huddled safely under the branches of one of the nearby pine trees. At first he panicked when he could not find his wife, but soon he saw Sophia, down on her hands and knees again, without her gloves on, searching every inch of her surroundings for little Timmy. Her voice was hoarse from calling his name. Oliver's heart sank deeper in his chest.

He quickly approached and pulled his freezing wife to her feet. He looked at her tear-stained face and told her to put her skis back on. She looked up at him with a puzzled look, "But why?! We can't--! We can't leave Timmy!!" He understood her pleas but told her that they had to move quickly down to the base of the mountain, for it was their only chance to get help. He was the leader of their family and, although his heart broke for his wife, he was not about to lose her, too.

As before, Oliver broke off tree branches and heavily marked the area where they believed Timmy was set down. Before they could change their minds, Oliver took Sophia's hand and pulled her along behind him and they descended the mountain. As they skied away, tears of complete devastation poured down Oliver's and Sophia's faces. Fortunately neither one could see the other crying.

They both felt like they were abandoning their precious son and, even worse, they may never see him again. The thought was absolutely unbearable. Would they ever hold his little hand again? Would they ever kiss his smiling face?

At that moment, unbeknownst to his distraught parents, little Timmy was safe and sound, tucked away in a cozy cave on the side of Aspen Mountain.

PART TWO

Timmy softly snored in his deep sleep, completely oblivious to his surroundings or the fact that he had been separated from his mother and father. His friendly and furry rescuers crowded around him in a circle staring in awe at the soft little creature they had stumbled upon at the side of the trail, buried beneath mounds of snow. As they stared at the little boy, still secure in his sturdy bag thing, they were delighted to realize that they had a new playmate of their very own. He was the newest addition to their unique and close-knit family.

For the few furry family members who weren't there, the others recalled with great drama how this wonderful twist of fate happened. Late afternoon was a normally a special time of day in the mountain forest which they all enjoyed. They were free to romp and play in the snow once all the strange people with the peculiar things attached to their faces, hands, and feet stopped intruding on their beloved playground for the day. The snowstorm, which always seemed to chase the people off the mountain, was a welcome sight to the animals. Emma, the pure white bunny with the most spectacular violet eyes, was rolling around and around in the fresh powder of the new snowfall as her friendly brother Matthew the brave and colorful blue jay, sung delightful tunes of happiness around her ears. Suddenly, their trusty and protective group leader, Tyler, lumbered up to them. Tyler was an enormous black mountain bear known as much for his kindness as he was for his size.

Tyler grumbled to Emma and Matthew that it was getting late and close to their bedtime. He was telling them to follow him home, but they weren't really listening and Emma continued to roll around and around in the soft snow. Suddenly they all heard a big clunk as Tyler hit an unfamiliar object with one of his giant back paws and pushed it over. Matthew, with his bird's eye view, told the startled Emma that Tyler hadn't knocked over a branch or a rock, but a living creature in a bag that was now making strange noises. With extreme curiosity, they all quickly hurried over to see what all the fuss was about.

As they stumbled up to the unfamiliar object, they discovered it was a huge pack that was pushed over to the very edge of the massive mountain and was about to fall off the ridge at any moment. It was perched on a ledge under the trail above. "Where did it come from?" Emma said. She approached the edge of the strange bundle but, with lightning speed and agility, Tyler stopped Emma in her tracks as Matthew hovered above. Tyler's ears tilted upward

where they heard voices on the trail. Frantic, frenzied people voices shouting. What was going on? Emma couldn't worry about that right now; she had to focus her attention on this mystery bundle. Tyler feared any sudden movement would send him, Emma and the strange bag over the edge. He called upon Matthew to fly down over the big bag that was resting on its side and report back what he saw. Matthew, who was flattered to be so indispensable to Tyler, took this important assignment very seriously. He flew his reconnaissance mission through the snow and wind and reported back that the "package" was very close to falling off the side of the mountain. The slightest movement could mean the end of whatever was inside it.

Emma exclaimed, "I am going over there right now to rescue the prize that we found!" Tyler effortlessly scooped the excited bunny up in his giant paw, which was the size of a dinner plate, and held her close. He calmly said, "Emma, I know you want to rescue whatever is in that bag, but we need to be very careful because any movement could cause the bag to fall over the edge. And I don't know what I would do if anything ever happened to you."

Emma took Tyler's advice and quickly came up with Plan B. She looked up at Tyler and said, "I have an idea. What if we tie branches together and have Matthew fly over and attach the branch rope to the bottom of the bag?" Tyler looked at her skeptically. "Once our tightrope is securely fastened and in place," she continued, "we can carefully pull it back toward us until it is safe." Tyler actually thought this plan might work. They all quickly gathered Aspen branches and fastened them together. Finally, they had a very long and secure tightrope. They then called upon the blue jay to clutch the end of the tightrope in his two feet, fly over to the bundle, and fasten the makeshift rope to it. Matthew did as he was told and soon the mission was accomplished. The proud blue jay flew back to inform his friends that it was now okay to start pulling.

Ever so slowly, Tyler and Emma pulled branch after Aspen branch, struggling against the weight of the mystery bag on the other end. Finally, they felt the bundle giving way, which they took as a good sign. It was now out of the ditch that it was buried in and at the very edge of the mountain. But they knew that they had to be extremely careful so as not to lose their grip for fear that the little bundle would tumble over the mountain's edge. Tyler instructed Emma and Matthew to continue to gently and slowly pull the homemade tightrope toward them as he anchored it like someone in the game of tug-o-war. They did as he asked and soon the trio was able to pull the bundle to safety!

Once the curious bag was safely lying beside them, the exhausted creatures looked at one another, wondering what to do next. They were filled with curiosity about the strange creature, but with fear as well, when the odd bundle started to whimper. This sound was foreign to their ears. After a moment, brave Emma hopped over to the bag and, with her furry paws, slowly pulled the blanket back. To their wonder and surprise, they all laid their eyes upon the most splendid sight. Inside the bundle lay a precious little human with round, rosy cheeks and the most sparkling blue eyes. These eyes stared back at them, equally as curious.

All of a sudden, the blue eyed mini-human let out a wide mouthed scream of fear and confusion. This caused Emma to do the same. Tyler and Matthew were quick to follow. In no time the four of them were screaming as loud as they could. Oddly, this caused the small human to actually stop screaming. He searched Emma's eyes with his own. Emma realized that the boy was terribly scared and extremely cold. Tyler rose up on his hind legs, making him larger than life, and gently bent down and scooped the bundle into his warm arms. Matthew took this as a sign that it was time to go home, so he cheerfully took flight and led the way back to the cave.

Once they were deep inside their home, Tyler set the bundle down with great care. Now the little boy peered out from the blanket he had pulled up to his face and saw that he was surrounded by, not only the three strange creatures who miraculously came to his rescue, but dozens of creatures of all shapes and sizes. I must be dreaming, little Timmy thought. He closed his eyes with a soft expression on his

face, and once again dozed off. He wasn't really scared anymore, but he just wanted this strange dream to finish so he could wake up in his mother's loving arms.

Meanwhile, as the strange little boy soundly slept, the animals who had found each other, one by one, upon this majestic mountain and become a big loving family, huddled silently around the boy with a sense of pride, protectiveness, and excitement. They all realized that they had found a precious addition to their happy clan.

They were the oddest of families, for not one of them resembled the other. Perhaps this is what made them so unique. Each had an amazing gift or ability, distinctly different from one another, which enabled them to understand that differences can lead to unconditional love and acceptance too. They knew that you didn't have to look alike to love one another.

Besides Tyler, Emma, and Matthew, the clan also included Madeleine, the incredibly kind and nurturing mountain lamb; Jack, the free-spirited, humorous and handsome golden stallion; Lenny, the wise, strong and confident mountain lion; Cao, the fiercely protective and cunning coyote; Hunter, the wise, insightful and mountain goat; Jade, the cuddly, energetic and vivacious chipmunk, Christian, the intelligent, courageous and playful Bernese Mountain Dog; Tessa, the bashful, inquisitive and exotic-looking doe; and, of course, Lyla, the adorable, spirited, and resilient kitten.

The animals continued to closely huddle about the sleeping boy through the evening, the night, and into the wee hours of the morning. As dawn approached and a ray of light pierced the opening of the grand cave which they all proudly called home, the animals started to disperse in order to go about their early morning chores. Some cleaned, some organized, and some hunted for their day's food with delight for today was going to be a special day. Today they were going to celebrate the arrival of the newest addition to their family.

Madeleine and Emma started a little fire in preparation for their morning meal and set the water filled kettle upon it. Christian, Tessa and Lyla set out on a little journey to pick fresh nuts and berries, while Matthew joyfully flew about them singing his delightful songs. Meanwhile, Lenny and Cao headed up the mountain in search of sticks and leaves to keep the fire going. From the entrance to the cave, Jack galloped across the beautiful mountain terrain in one direction, and Tyler proudly strode the other way to make sure that there were no passersby who might get too close to their home. He knew there was nothing like a bear sighting to make a human change direction!

As Madeleine and Emma were busy stirring the pot of oats and porridge in the boiling kettle, they were startled by a very loud, high pitched and sustained screeching sound. They turned at once to check on the sleeping little boy to make sure that he was safe before investigating the sound; only to realize that the noises were actually coming from the tiny boy's very big mouth!

They quietly walked over to him, both overwhelmed with a sense of protectiveness. As they approached the strange little creature with the peculiar sounds coming from his mouth, what they witnessed next literally stopped them in their tracks. The little boy, still securely bundled within his blanket and with only his tiny face peering out. But that face was completely red! It was almost the color of fire, as he screamed hysterically.

Madeleine carefully made her way closer as Emma hopped alongside her. They now realized that once this little boy had awakened from his slumber, he must have been very confused about where he was and he must be missing his mother and father terribly. They each remembered this fretful feeling from when they were younger and they, too, were lost, only to be found by their new loving family. They also realized this little boy must be very hungry. Their hearts went out to him and they were as determined as ever to comfort him, protect him, and most of all, to love him.

In hope of calming the child, Emma hopped even closer. Madeleine began to gently unwrap the little bundle from his pack with her delicate hooves. The curious little boy stared up in absolute fear, and his eyes grew larger and larger as his cries became louder and louder.

The other family members had been rushing about the mountainside collecting food, water and supplies to welcome the new addition and celebrate the blessing of his unexpected arrival. When the sound of his cries filled the air, their protective instincts overcame them and they galloped, flew, ran and glided back to the cave. Once they arrived, they peeked their heads into the cave, one head on top of the other, from the smallest to the tallest family member. What they saw warmed their hearts.

The little boy, whom seconds before had been screaming out in panic, was now calmly and quietly cuddled in Madeleine's motherly embrace. Meanwhile, Emma was carefully and continuously shoveling spoonful after heaping spoonful of warm porridge into his gaping mouth.

As the other animals slowly made their way into the cave, the next sound they heard was delightful. It was the sound of giggling as the little boy beamed up at all of the funny and furry animals with a twinkle in his eyes and a rosy blush on his cheeks.

In his mind, this was just like the fully little stories his mother and father read to him night after night; fully of colorful and silly characters. In his wildest dreams he never could have imagined that all the creatures in those lovely stories would actually come to life and play with him.

From that moment on, the tiny child became a cherished part of their special and unique family.

Little Timmy grew, blossomed and thrived under their constant watchfulness in an outside world full of kindness, loyalty and unconditional love.

PART THREE

As time passed, the little boy, whom his new family decided to name Sebastian because they didn't know what else he was called, continued to grow and thrive in their care. He passed the days riding on Jack's big back with his fingers wrapped in the horse's mane, singing the silly songs that Matthew taught him, and learning how to stay safe in the forest.

Little Sebastian was developing his own unique personality and he was a constant source of delight to his proud family. He loved them with all his heart. Sometimes, though, when he snuggled with Emma after Madeleine had tucked them in, the little boy had dreams of a beautiful, golden-haired someone who would hold him closely as she sang to him in the loveliest voice, and a tall handsome someone who would gaze at him with eyes full of love. Whenever the little boy had these visions, he would awaken with a smile upon his lips, peace within his heart, but confusion in his mind.

Sebastian loved his big family, but inside he felt a deep yearning for something that was missing. He kept these thoughts and feelings to himself, though, because he didn't want to trouble Emma, Madeleine, Tyler and the others.

But what he didn't know was that his furry family sensed that he felt out of place. They never failed to take notice when the normally carefree and fun loving boy became quiet and reflective. It made them sad to see him that way, but no one dared tell him that he wasn't quite one of them or that they rescued him from the edge of the mountain one snowy day. They feared that sharing the truth would somehow cause them to lose the boy they cherished so much.

While their family thrived on the side of beautiful Aspen mountain, in the picturesque town below a kind, sweet, but sad French couple tried to live one day at a time in their new reality.

PART FOUR

Oliver and Sophia, now lived in the charming little town of Aspen. They owned and operated a local art gallery which brought great talent and joy to all of the town's locals, as well as to all the tourists, famous and otherwise, who frequented the resort town.

They were known and adored by all. They hosted the most talked-about galas and gallery events, which were always praised by the local media. Their gallery, which they named Timothy's Gallery, was full of exquisite paintings, sculptures, jewelry and hand-crafted relics by both world-renown artists as well as the talented local artists. Upon entering Timothy's Gallery, celebrities and locals alike instantly knew that they had entered another world, an old world, for they were undeniably drawn in by its wonder and its beauty.

It was only when one had the rare opportunity to truly get to know Sophia and Oliver, or to the keen and discriminating eye of a certain artist or collector, that one detected the void and sadness that enveloped them. It was also seen in the slight look of longing that was deep in their eyes and hearts. Although they were perfect hosts to all who entered their gallery, they still kept customers and friends at a discreet distance.

Often times, visitors to Aspen would wander into the beautiful gallery and strike up a conversation with the owners. Unaware of Oliver and Sophia's tragic story, they would usually ask if they had any children. Oliver and Sophia would look into one another's eyes with a depth and an utter devastation that only the two of them would ever share or completely comprehend, and politely answer all the questions with this simple response: "We love our gallery. It keeps us very busy. We love to be here each and every day, for you never know what wonder will walk through the door."

Although they found it hard to remain in the very town in which they lost little Timmy, Oliver and Sophia knew that deep inside their souls, their longing for their precious little boy would never go away and that they would never ever give up the hope of finding him. They could never imagine letting him down again by leaving him. Their love for their child, combined with their unwavering determination to never give up hope that he would return to them, kept them tethered to this town no matter what.

Whenever they had a quiet moment alone, they would revisit the chain of events that led to the loss of their son atop Aspen Mountain and the rescue effort that followed.

Even though the authorities called off their search for their baby after only a few days, the parents' search continued on for years.

Two long years ago, on top of Aspen Mountain, a day that began with sheer excitement had ended in tragedy. It is a day they continually replayed in their minds, always searching for a different ending. The local news had called the blizzard the worst storm in Aspen's history.

The night of the storm, Oliver had finally convinced his wife to come with him, above her sobs that she could not leave the site where their son had disappeared. They finally headed off together in search for help. In vain, they spread a trail of branches behind them as they continued farther away from the site of Timmy's disappearance. They were determined to get onto the main ski trail as fast as they could in search of someone who could help them. Deep inside they knew this was the only way they could rescue their boy.

At last, they saw the trail they sought which ran down to the base of Aspen Mountain. Although they had descended it several times earlier in the day with Timmy, it now looked different through the driving snow and their weary eyes. Darkness had fallen and all the other skiers had already found their way safely down the trail hours earlier. Oliver figured that the ski patrol had almost certainly conducted their final safety inspection of the day; satisfied that no skiers or snow boarders remained on the mountain.

He did not want to share his trepidations with Sophia for fear that she would instinctively flee back to the spot where they had last seen their son. Instead, he firmly gripped her hand in an attempt to comfort her and give her encouragement to continue on. But the massive blizzard was impeding their progress in every possible way. There was so much fresh powder now that it proved even more difficult than they could have imagined to make any headway. They'd hoped to reach Buddha's Restaurant and the ski patrol shack, which were both located midway down the mountain. After over an hour of skiing and enduring the early signs of frostbite, they were very relieved when the restaurant and shack appeared in the near distance.

With a surge of hope, they pushed forward using every ounce of strength they could muster. For now they knew they were mere moments away from finding the help they so desperately needed. As they approached the buildings, Oliver quickly snapped out of his ski binding and raced through the snow so deep that it threatened to swallow him. Closing the distance between the two, Sophia had almost caught up with Oliver just as he reached the door of the ski patrol shack and threw it open. "Help! We've lost our baby on the mountain," he hollered before he realized the room was completely empty.

Sophia burst through the door panting seconds later and took in the sight of the deserted building. Any hope that remained of finding the help they urgently needed melted like their footprints on the tile floor. Sophia fell to her knees in utter disbelief. "What now?" she cried to Oliver as hot tears spilled down her frozen cheeks. "I can't leave my sweet boy outside in this storm! I'm going back to find him!"

Oliver knelt down in front of his wife and held her freezing hands in his. Attempting to share his strength with her through their fingers he squeezed her tight and said, "We must first check the restaurant next door to see if there is anyone left. If not, then we will have no choice. We must continue to the base of the mountain to find help." Sophia protested, but Oliver explained that they could never make it back up the mountain in the face of this brutal weather. "What good would we be to Timmy when he is found if we are killed or injured?" Oliver could also not bear the thought of letting his wife out of his sight. "Come on now. We must go as fast as we can." Sophia let Oliver pull her up and they hurried outside, reattaching their skis and making their way over to Buddha's Restaurant, dimly lit by the blowing string of Christmas lights encircling the deck. Once again snapping out of his bindings, Oliver left Sophia at the base of the steps to take a quick look inside. His fears were again realized when he looked around the empty room. Suddenly overtaken with complete hopelessness and suffocating guilt, he fell to the floor and wept into his hands. He had to face the reality that he was not the protector he had prided himself on being. He had let his family down in the most devastating way. He was responsible for losing their child, now he feared Sophia might be injured by the harsh weather and plummeting temperatures. How could this have happened? How could *he* have let this happen? He felt he had devastated his beloved family by placing them all at risk.

With this thought in his mind, he realized what he had to do. He had to gather his wits about him and come up with another rescue plan. The first step was to get to his feet and be the man he believed himself to be. No more time for self-pity, he thought. He rose to his full height and looked around once again. This time, however, he was not focused on what wasn't there, but rather on what *was* there. Instead of seeing only isolation and emptiness, Oliver saw more. He saw brightness in the ceiling lights and table candles, he saw warmth and reprieve from the storm in the fireplace and stack of wood beside it, and he saw sustenance in the restaurant's kitchen. In other words, he saw a safe haven in which Sophia could reside in while he continued his search for help.

He was reenergized with his new plan and set about lighting candles, starting a fire, and pulling food from the shelves. As he was rushing about building a sanctuary of warmth and nourishment, Sophia silently entered the cabin. As she did, she was overwhelmed; first by the warmth and then by the realization of what her husband was doing. He was sacrificing himself to save her, to rescue their son, and to reunite their family.

Once Oliver had his wife tucked safely away and out of the bitter cold, he gently kissed her on the forehead and wrapped her in his strong arms. After releasing her, he walked out the door of Buddha's Restaurant as tears slid down his face. He hated leaving her alone, but he was confident that she was safe and he had made the right decision. The only decision, really, for this was the only way to reach help in time.

Oliver found his skis, snapped back in and, saying a silent prayer, pushed off down the steep main trail of Ajax Mountain.

After several hours of battling the blizzard conditions, he was grateful when the snowfall began to slow and he could finally see the bright lights aglow beyond him in the near distance. It was a sight for his sore eyes. The lights he saw belonged to the town of Aspen, alive with activity and dining despite the weather. He drew a deep breath and looked up into the sky, once again alight with twinkling stars and moon, and thanked God for guiding him to safety and the help that he needed so desperately.

For the very first time since losing Timothy on the mountain and embarking on a terrifying journey of desperation, Oliver suddenly felt somewhat triumphant. He sped down the last leg of the mountain's trail with record breaking speed and quickly glided to the base of the mountain where the gondolas had been tucked in to ride out the storm – to the exact point where they had started their day, a family day that enough fun and happiness to last a lifetime.

The day had taken a terrible turn, but Oliver was more determined than ever to make sure that it did not end in tragedy. This was his job as the protector. He took off his skis and raced down the steps beside the gondolas which led to the office of the Ski Patrol. As he burst through the door, a very young man looked up from his desk in surprise. All the skiers had retired for the day and were currently out and about enjoying the nightlife of Aspen, or safely tucked into their beds after witnessing the dramatic snowstorm that afternoon. All of the other ski patrol officers had left hours earlier, once they were certain that everyone was safely off the mountain. As Oliver stared around the huge empty office, he felt a surge of anger that the army of rescuers he had envisioned to be waiting for him were nowhere to be found – only a young many barely old enough to shave. Where was the search party that should be gathering to search for Oliver and his family? Did anyone care? As these thoughts raced through his mind, he suddenly realized that no one actually knew that they were lost. How could they have known? For, in fact, they were from a foreign country with no family or community ties to Aspen. Who would have reported them missing? No one.

They had been the ones who had chosen to tackle the massive and sometimes dangerous mountain themselves, without a professional seasoned guide. William, who had started them out on their grand adventure with the appropriate gear and the warning about the impending storm, was the only one who would have known they were there. No one else knew them, or where they were going, or where they might be at the moment.

Oliver refused to waste another second on these useless thoughts and rushed forward to the desk. He ordered the young patrolman to pick up the telephone and contact the chief officer to organize an emergency rescue party ASAP to look for his missing son. The patrolman was stunned by the appearance of this man with the accent who had just busted through the doors of the office. His cheeks were flushed, he had holes poked throughout his expensive ski suit, and he had scratches and bruises covering his gloveless hands. But the most shocking part of his appearance was his face for it contained a look of fear, despair and horror the likes of which the young man had never seen before. That alone set the adrenaline loose in his body and he sprang into action. He quickly picked up the phone, nervously thumbed through a stack of papers trying to find his boss's phone number and pushed in the digits with his shaking hands.

When he heard the alert but tired voice on the other end of the line, the young patrolman's throat dried out. He had just awoken the Lieutenant in the middle of the night. He couldn't imagine what his punishment would be or how much he would be harassed by the veteran patrolmen if it turned out that this man's extraordinary story wasn't true.

He rapidly rambled into the phone, stuttering and stumbling over simple words in his nervousness. Oliver, exploding with impatience, grabbed the phone from the boy's grasp and barked orders into the line.

Within 20 minutes, the ski patrol office was filled with dozens of people in various uniforms. As word had spread through the emergency channels of the small town, police officers, firefighters, paramedics, and even civilians showed up to offer help. The hastily organized search party consisted of over 100 Aspenites. Word of the potential tragedy that had befallen the visiting French family had spread like wildfire throughout the town. People began rushing in from near and far to offer their assistance. Oliver was deeply touched as he stood in the corner of the Ski Patrol Lieutenant's office. As he hurriedly answered the Lieutenant's questions, he also watched the crowd of people gathering at this very late hour to help. The night air was full of flashing lights, blazing sirens and the human electricity of excitement and organization. The rescue team that Oliver and Sophia had hoped and prayed for hours earlier was finally forming before his eyes. But was it already too late?

Though clusters of low clouds still moved quickly across the night sky, the snow had completely stopped.

There was a guide at the main entrance of the ski patrol office shouting orders and organizing the growing group of volunteers according to their expertise. Expert skiers, seasoned patrol officers, and EMTs circled the gondola loading deck waiting for the operators to get the massive chairlift system back online and moving up the massive 10,750-foot mountain. A group of Aspen locals, who had grown up in the town skiing every inch of the mountain, gathered their ski equipment and hurried to the base. A group of older folks manned the radios and made coffee for the search and rescue people who were still waiting in the office for their instructions. Later, more townspeople would bring baked goods and hearty soups to feed the growing group of volunteers searching for the poor lost French boy.

As assignments were being handed out, Lieutenant Charles took Oliver by the arm and guided him to a private corner. He looked him square in the eyes and, with a squeeze of his arm, assured him that they would find Timothy and bring both mother and son safely off the mountain. Oliver nodded a silent thank you and the Lieutenant stepped away and blew the horn signaling that the time had come for all groups to get busy with their responsibilities. Then the Lieutenant pulled on his hat and gloves and headed out with his chin down to brace himself against the bitter cold.

The gondola operators had rushed back to the mountain's base to help in the effort. They quickly got the lifts working just as Lieutenant Charles reached the operator's booth. To his dismay, as he was about to board the first gondola, a now familiar voice behind him called out, "Wait!! I'm coming!" Charles turned in the direction of the voice, but he already knew it belonged to the lost boy's father.

Concerned that Oliver had already been exposed to the elements for a dangerous amount of time and was actually showing signs of frostbite, hypothermia and dehydration, Charles firmly instructed Oliver to return to the ski patrol building and await news. Oliver brushed by Charles as if he hadn't heard a word and squeezed onto the crowded pod. His entire life was up there on that mountain and no one was going to keep him from going back up. This infuriated the man who was used to having his orders followed. He barked at Oliver, "Get off the gondola and go back inside. You are too weak and injured to be of any help. You will only get in the way up there and slow us down!"

But his admonition fell on deaf ears as Oliver stood inside the gondola clutching his ski equipment and yelled out to the man in the control booth to send them on their way up.

Deep down, Charles knew that any father and husband worth his salt would do the same so his protests dwindled and his admiration increased for this determined Frenchman.

Both men rode up in silence. Each tried to be hopeful, but Oliver knew how long it had been since he'd last seen Timothy, and Charles knew what the unforgiving mountain could do to a little boy. For the second time that day, Oliver ascended Ajax. The big differences between his two trips was that this time his family was not there.

Behind them, gondola after gondola was filled with expert skiers impatient to reach the top so they could begin their descent and find the boy. All were eager to find him. All believed they may be too late. No one spoke; each lost in their own thoughts; each thinking how glad they were that their own loved ones were safe at home.

Oliver and Charles reached the top of the mountain just as the skies were beginning to lighten. Pod after pod arrived at the top and emptied their human cargo onto the platform. The crowd of rescuers gathered awaiting their direct orders from the Lieutenant. Most were surprised to see the father of the lost boy standing to the Lieutenant's right. They were all touched by his devotion and determination to save his family. His strong and confident presence quickly erased any doubts the search party had and created an atmosphere of hope.

The large search party continued on well into the magnificent dawn marked by a breathtaking sunrise over Aspen Mountain. They covered every trail, every cavern, every back country route, every rest stop, cabin and restaurant located on the mountain. Every square foot of the massive mountain was combed for signs of the small boy. Hope remained, as unlikely as it was, that they boy had been found by other skiers who then hunkered down in a safe place with him to await rescue. The sunrise brought with it warming temperatures and the brightness of a new day.

Charles radioed for all group leaders to assemble their teams and meet him right away at Buddha's Restaurant halfway down the mountain – the spot where Sophia had been left to await news.

Within less than a half an hour the entire search party had reconvened inside the warmth of Buddha's Restaurant. Oliver was disappointed when he heard Charles issue the order to pull in the search party. It took all his strength not to object when he knew that every second mattered and they should be spending them looking for Timothy. He worried that the group meeting was a sign that the Lieutenant had given up and was suspending the search for his son. The only silver lining was the knowledge that

Sophia had heeded his advice and stayed in the warmth and safety of Buddha's Restaurant. But as he walked through the doors of the restaurant, his eyes made a quick search of the space but could not spot Sophia. He instantly began to panic.

William, the young man who served as the French family's ski outfitter and tour guide merely 24 hours earlier now stood in the mountaintop restaurant among the other volunteers. He saw the distress on Oliver's face and rushed to his side to explain to him that his wife was safe. In fact, when William's rescue group arrived ahead of Oliver, they were surprised to find the lights on in the restaurant and a blazing fire alight in the massive fireplace. But they were even more surprised to find a woman asleep in front of it. William instantly recognized her as the French woman from the day before. Unbelievably, the exhausted woman had slept through the heavy sound of a dozen boots climbing the outside stairs. He had crossed the floor and gently squeezed Sophia shoulder so as not to startle her. When Sophia opened her eyes she felt like she was in a dream. A small group of men and women surrounded her. They were completely clad in ski gear from head to toe. When she saw the somewhat familiar face of William, she realized this was no dream at all. This was the search party that Oliver had promised her he would bring; the one she fell asleep praying for. That prayer had been answered! She sprung up crying, "Dieu! Merci!! Timothy! Here I am! Mommy is here! I'm so sorry!" Her frantic words continued on and on as she ran all about the large cabin in a manic search for her rescued son. She ran out to the back deck when she didn't find him inside amongst the strangers. It was then that the cold realization rushed over her again. Timmy was still missing.

William and Oliver met her as she reentered the restaurant. With heartbreaking dread Oliver knew what he had to do. He had to tell Sophia that their son was still on the mountain. He had to tell her that the search and rescue party had been unable their find her boy. He had to tell her that he had failed his family. Instead he stepped forward and enveloped Sophia in his strong arms. In her husband's crushing embrace, Sophia knew what he could not say. Her prayers had not been answered. The search party was not there to return her boy to her. They had come in because they had given up. They had called off the search party and left her son to freeze to death upon their so-called "Magical Mountain".

Sophia struggled to free herself of Oliver's tightening embrace. When he would not release her she pounded his back with one fist while clutching the gold baby booties charm around her neck with her other hand. That charm which she received from Oliver just before they embarked on this vacation, symbolized the best part of her life. The horrible cries now came from deep within her; from a place she had never known existed. They hung in the air to be heard by all, within the restaurant and beyond.

And two years later, those cries of anguish, despair and pain lived on in the hearts and souls of not just Oliver and Sophia, but in those of the search party and townspeople who were all part of the French family's private and public tragedy.

PART FIVE

Sebastian was such a happy and easy going young boy and he was thriving in his home with his silly and loving family. Over the last two years, they had built a secure haven for him on the outskirts of Aspen Mountain. They provided him with nourishment, adoration, and even a bit of adventure here and there; but always under their watchful eyes. Sebastian was their pride and joy, and he knew it. He always tried to obey the strict rules of the family leader, Tyler, and the family matriarchs, Madeleine and Emma. However, he began to feel that their rules were stricter for him. Although he felt protected, he also felt confined and isolated. He dutifully went about his daily chores of collecting berries, water, food, and twigs for the fire. At times, other chores allowed for him to venture a little farther away from the haven of their cozy cave and explore new terrain. But at the end of each day, after they all enjoyed each other's company and shared the telling of their daily adventures, Sebastian started to feel a twinge of confinement and jealousy. He knew his furry family loved him deeply, but he was growing up and was beginning to feel overprotected compared to his other siblings. Being the free spirited little boy that he was raised to be, and always being a constant source of humor to his family, he now felt the need to spread his wings and come up with new adventures during the day that he, too, could share with the others at night.

Madeleine seemed to sense a restlessness in Sebastian that she had never seen before. One night, as she tucked him into bed, she looked deep into his eyes and asked him if he was okay. He shook off her concern and replied that everything was just great and he was only tired from the days' activities. She kissed him goodnight on his forehead and left to join the others by the crackling fire at the mouth of the cave.

Even though Sebastian had promised her that he was okay, Madeleine knew that there was something bothering the little boy. She shared her concerns with all the others and they all began to worry. They talked amongst themselves in hushed voices. They worried that maybe he was starting to remember his past; was starting to realize that they were not, in fact, his real family; was remembering his real parents. They feared that he would one day leave them forever, but hoped that would never happen.

Emma silently left the concerned little group gathered by the fire and quietly snuck into bed beside Sebastian. She wrapped her soft, white bunny paws around him as she had done each night for the past two years. She always wanted to protect and love him and she knew she would do anything in her power to make sure he was safe and happy. As he slept, she quietly examined the tiny little bracelet for the thousandth time. He had been wearing it since the day they found him. Although they had to add some string to it to accommodate his growing wrist, it was still beautiful.

Sebastian, who was, in fact, not sleeping at all, tried to pretend to be so as not to break the rules. He loved sleeping with the warm and kind bunny Emma. Her snuggles comforted him and he couldn't remember sleeping any other way. When she wrapped her furry paws around him, he always felt better. But not tonight. It seemed that nothing could chase away the restlessness he felt. He longed to spread his wings far and wide. He longed for adventure. Without meaning to, he let out a deep sigh. Emma sat up and looked straight in the little boy's eyes. When he opened his eyes and met her gaze, Emma saw the deep look of sadness within them. She hugged him close and softly whispered, "Do not fret little one. Tomorrow will be an amazing new day filled with great promise. And as a special little treat for you, I will take you with me on my daily chores, which will be a bright new adventure for you. It will be great fun, but it has to be our little secret. Now close your eyes and dream of a wonderful new day."

Without saying a word, Sebastian closed his eyes and drifted off. He smiled in his sleep because he realized that Emma understood.

That next morning, after a hearty breakfast, Emma joined Madeleine and Joyous Jade in the kitchen to wash the dishes and stack the makeshift cooler with the morning's leftovers. She then excused herself saying she was off to gather fresh fruits and berries for the day and may even venture into town to see if she could find any delicious scraps of baked goods she could bring back for their dinner that night. They wished her good luck and Emma quickly hopped away.

Normally, at this time of day, Sebastian could be found outside the mouth of the cave singing silly songs or doing somersaults in the patch of wildflowers to amuse Matthew and Hunter. Emma called out to her reliable travel companion Jack, the handsome stallion, who happily galloped over to her side. Ever the gentleman, he bowed low to the ground so that Emma could hop aboard. As the pair began to trot away from the cave, Emma whispered into Jack's giant ear and asked him to slow down a bit and stop over by the tall rock ahead of them which was surrounded by beautiful high grass and blooming flowers. Jack was confused but he did as he was asked. As they approached the rock Emma hopped off and disappeared into the tall grass. Jack was even more surprised to see her emerge moments later with Sebastian by her side. The confused horse bent down once again and the pair climbed upon him. Matthew joined the group and the foursome headed away. Adventure was clearly in the air.

It was a spectacular spring day as the excited group of four made their way down the mountainside. Sebastian was in complete awe of his surroundings as they descended the mountain they called home and made their way closer to the town of Aspen. He had heard many nighttime tales about the travels and adventures of his furry and feathered family beyond the safety of the cave, but he had never experienced any of it himself. His vivid imagination had painted a picture for him, but it did not do justice to what he saw now. The massive mountain terrain, with all of its trails and valleys, stretched out before him far and wide. The rapidly blooming array of flowers provided a breathtaking backdrop and an intoxicating scent. The buzzing, chattering and chirping of other animals who populated the mountain was a surprise to him, for he thought that his furry family members were the only ones that lived there. The many babbling streams which ran down the mountainside carrying melted snow from the summit were amazing, and the funny little carts that traveled up and down the mountain on a cable wire looked like little flying saucers. Saucers in the sky!

Suddenly Sebastian let out a cry of surprise when he heard and then saw something that was so foreign and completely shocking to him. Jack, who was gracefully galloping down the side of the mountain on the hidden trails they normally traveled to stay out of sight of the humans who traversed the mountains all year long, came to a sudden halt at the boy's exclamation. Emma turned suddenly about from her position in front of the boy. The chirping blue jay, Matthew, also stopped flying around and joined them upon the stallion's back. As they all looked at the little boy, they saw that he was in a daze as he stared in wonder at the human beings, rigorously and happily hiking up the side of the mountain, laughing and chatting away to one another.

And then something happened that would change their family forever.

Watching the hikers as they passed, Sebastian's face erupted into smile and he whispered, almost to himself, "Mama? Papa?" And something that he couldn't quite put his little finger on fluttered in his memory.

Emma quickly instructed Jack to move over behind the tall Aspen trees so as to hide them from view. Jack did as he was told and the foursome waited in silence as the hikers continued their steady climb up the mountainside. Sebastian continued to stare in awe of these strange, but familiar creatures. He took in every single detail of their being, from the clothes that they wore to their faces, arms, legs, ears, fingers, to the sounds coming from their mouths.

They had no fur. They had no feathers. Just like him. As he stared in fascination, the little boy realized that he was more similar to these foreign creatures, than he was to his own family members. It seemed so odd to him, and although he had heard countless stories of "the humans" over the years, he had never expected them to look just like *him*.

After the hikers passed by them and continued to slowly progress up the trail out of earshot, the animals decided it was now safe to continue their descent.

Sebastian, still a bit stunned by the sight and sound of the humans, and the thoughts they awakened in his mind, quickly pushed his worries away and was once again struck by the beauty around him. He did not want to miss even one moment or one minute detail of this awesome adventure that he had waited so long for.

Emma was also stunned. She was completely unprepared for Sebastian's loving reaction to seeing strangers. Her little mind became awash with the emotions of the life that Sebastian had before they found him that one snowy afternoon.

Unaware of Emma's thoughts, the rest of the journey down "Ajax" Mountain was quite an adventure for the little boy. It was filled with majestic scenery, tons of fun and laughter and even a bit of excitement as Jack galloped at an amazing speed through the difficult twists and curves of the mountain terrain, with Sebastian gripping tightly to his thick mane.

Completely caught up in the excitement of this wonderful and unexpected adventure, little Sebastian almost missed the most remarkable view of the journey altogether. It was not until Emma turned around and smiled at him, as Matthew cheerily chirped above, and Jack's gallop came to a slow and steady trot, that the boy looked straight ahead and saw something that took his breath. His jaw dropped open as he set his eyes upon the charming town of Aspen. And what a view it was to behold.

Jack came to a standstill at the base of the mountain because he wanted to give the boy a chance to savor this moment and imprint it on his heart.

Sebastian's head was spinning as he looked this way and that. At first very quickly and then ever so slowly, as to take in every tiny detail of what he was witnessing.

As he looked before him, he took in the splendor of the village; from the tiny and colorful houses, almost like dollhouses, lining the small and tidy streets, to the horse and buggy carriages carrying humans--big ones and little ones *like him!* With the most contagious smiles upon their faces they walked to and from shops and restaurants. They climbed in and out of the funny little things that flew in the sky with all their odd gear. They strolled and biked along the streets. They reclined on patios and decks drinking and enjoying food that was foreign to his eyes, but smelled so delicious.

Little Sebastian was so overcome with the many splendors that he started to jump off the stallion's back, but not before Emma placed a protective paw on his arm to stop him from making a hasty, and possibly dangerous, move. At that moment, Emma looked deep into the little boy's eyes, a child that she longed to guide, protect and nurture at all costs. But the truth of the matter was that they all---and no one more intensely than Emma herself—felt that they were risking the unimaginable; losing their precious little boy forever.

She knew this may be a possibility when she reluctantly promised to grant little Sebastian his dream of finally joining them on one of their many adventures. Even though the true and painful reality was that he was just inches and moments away from discovering the real world outside of their simple home. She could never bear the thought that the little cherished boy may be lost to them forever. But she knew she could no longer hold him back from experiencing more in life than just their very secluded home. She had finally given in to his pleas and was granting Sebastian his grandest dream of all. But this gift came at a tremendous cost to his family who raised him, coddled him, protected him, and loved him with every single breath they took; truly the only family the little boy ever remembered.

Emma looked into Sebastian's bright and naïve eyes. She saw that they were filled with overwhelming trust, excitement and love, and she instantly knew what she must do.

Although she would inevitably have to pay the price by answering to her other family members, Emma's unconditional love for the little boy overcame her. And she knew without a doubt that she must let him go and give him the chance to thrive, to spread his wings, and to explore all of the amazing gifts, adventures and dreams that life could offer to him, but that her little family could not.

They could continue to protect, nurture, and love him, but they could never give him everything that, as a human, he deserved. They did the best they could and it was now time for him to flourish and grow with the tools, the values and the unconditional love that they had so happily bestowed upon him since that joyous day they found him on the mountain. As much as it pained Emma's little heart, she tried to remember that Sebastian's human mother must also have a broken heart from losing him.

So Emma bravely and gently released her protective grip on little Sebastian's arm and let him go.

With a lump in her throat she whispered, "It is okay my darling boy, you must go live the life you were meant to." The little boy looked up at her with wide eyed curiosity and confusion, but she gently reassured him with a bright smile and a loving kiss on his soft cheek. Her whiskers tickled him, as they always did, and he touched his hand to his face where she had kissed him.

She told him that it was time for him to start his own adventure and that it was okay to go and join all the happy people in the beautiful and charming village. The little boy stood frozen in his spot as he looked at all the funny little creatures that were the only family, the only friends, and the only playmates he could clearly remember.

Tears of sadness and confusion filled his eyes and threatened to spill down when he was suddenly struck with the frightening thought that he was leaving them, or that, even worse, they were leaving him. Sensing the little boy's fear of being abandoned, but also sensing his excitement, Emma, Matthew, Jack, and Christian, unselfishly urged the boy to continue down the mountain, to spread his wings and to fly freely. They assured him that they would always be with him in his heart and that whether or not he saw them, they would always love and protect him. They would be proudly watching over him every step of his amazing journey.

Jack playfully leaned down and tousled the little boy's hair with his nose to bring a smile to Timmy's face. Then Christian licked his smiling face as a goodbye. Matthew, chirping above, gently came to rest on Sebastian's shoulder singing the beautiful little lullaby he used to sing to him when he was just a baby. The familiar sound of Matthew's tune instantly put Sebastian at ease and made him feel safe and loved.

And then Emma. With effort, and hiding most of the pain that weighed upon her heart, she hopped over to the boy's side. Sebastian bent down to hug her as she embraced him with all her furry might. When Sebastian opened his eyes, he looked into the distance and saw the magnificent sight of Tyler up on his hind legs as if waving him on. Sebastian saw it as the final sign he was waiting for that it was time to begin his adventure and leave his family behind for now.

The little boy, now seeming to have grown up instantly, started the remainder of his descent down the rugged mountain terrain; ever so slowly, and with a very heavy heart. But soon the sounds of talking and laughter from below beckoned him. Before he knew it, he was steadily bounding down the mountain until at last he reached its base.

Tyler, Emma, Matthew, Jack and Christian were glued to their spots, determined not to leave until they were sure their boy was safe. Soon the others—Tessa, Lyla, Madeleine, Cao, Hunter and Jade--joined them. The little group silently hovered on the side of the mountain. They felt the anguish of their collective loss, but also felt excitement for little Sebastian's newfound life. Deep down inside, they always knew they would have to let him go in order to allow him to live the life he was meant to have.

At the base of the mountain, beside the station where the gondolas arrived and departed all day long, a strapping young man named Adam stood. His job was to help the passengers safely embark and disembark from the gondolas. As Adam awaited an approaching group of tourists gliding down the cable in their pod, a rustling of trees along the trail caught his attention. As a member of the ski patrol and an avid hiker, Adam's first thought was that a starving grizzly bear was about to emerge from the woods. Every so often, the hungry giants would venture into town to raid the dumpsters in search of an easy meal. Adam knew he was the first line of defense to help protect the townspeople and tourists from the alarming but usually harmless visitor. Before Adam could even react, the source of the movement emerged. It turned out that it wasn't a bear at all. It was a beautiful little boy with a silver bracelet gleaming from his small wrist.

PART SIX

The little boy stared back at the strange human creature standing before him with the same bewilderment in his eyes that Adam had only moments before.

The child shrugged his shoulders, for he had certainly seen stranger things in his young life, and continued on his way. "What an adventure this is turning out to be! Now I have my own wild and fun story to report back to them. This is great! Won't my family be so proud of me for doing this on my own?" he thought to himself. Seeing the strange human (Adam) had only enhanced the little boy's curiosity. He knew there was more to his Big Adventure and, after all, he wanted his tales to be the greatest of all!

With only a threadbare shirt made out of fig leaves and Aspen pines, the little boy put one tiny bare foot in front of the other and set off.

Meanwhile, Adam, the awestruck ski patrol/summer guide just stared at the young boy as he continued on his journey. Adam was so accustomed to the stylish and elaborate attire of the Aspenites that it was very peculiar to see someone dressed so plainly. Adam instinctively knew something was not right.

He picked up the dispatch phone by the gondola station and called in to his lieutenant, Charles. He loudly and with much animation described the strange sight that he had just witnessed.

Charles listened intently on the other end of the line and agreed that Adam had indeed witnessed something odd. But in the far corners of his mind, something was gnawing at him. That something gave him a familiar and unsettling feeling, but he just could not quite put his finger on it. He told the young ski patrolman to keep an eye on the boy he would be right over. But when Adam hung up the phone and turned around, the boy was gone.

As Charles slowly hung up the telephone, as if he were handling some precious cargo, it slowly dawned on him why this sighting was so familiar. Suddenly all the memories started to flood back to him of a horrendous day two years ago.

A day that had haunted Charles ever since. He had proudly led the rescue team in search of the baby boy who had been separated from his parents, Oliver and Sophia. After dedicating countless hours, his entire heart, and his committed and loyal team to searching the mountaintop, Charles had had to make the most dreaded call of his entire life. For the safety of his team and their loved ones, he had called the search for the baby boy off. At the time, he had firmly believed that no one, let alone an innocent child, could have survived such a history-making snowstorm.

Charles himself believed in miracles; for a while he held out hope against the odds and even had vivid dreams that the helpless child had somehow survived and was nestled in a warm and safe place. Although most would consider it futile, Charles spent almost every day of the following year personally combing every inch of the unforgiving mountain for the little boy: every trail, every cave, and every crevice. Each time he ran into the lost little boy's parents in town, he became even more committed to finding their baby. The sorrow in their eyes motivated him every day of his yearlong search.

Charles prided himself on his loyalty, resourcefulness and compassion for humankind. If there was ever a mission that would be he true calling, this had been it. Being a beloved and devoted parent himself, how in the world could he ever let this French couple down? He was determined to reunite them with their baby.

As the days turned into months and the months turned into a year, even Charles began to acknowledge that his efforts to rescue Timmy, who had come to be known as "The Little Aspen Boy", were in vain. He would never forget the day he had to walk into Sophia and Oliver's art gallery to let them officially know that there was no longer any hope left of their son surviving. The looks of agony in their eyes were like daggers in his big heart.

The only thing Charles could think of to ease their pain and keep The Little Aspen Boy's memory alive was to dedicate a small and peaceful park, which sat beside the Rio Grande River in town, in Timmy's name. In the center of the park was placed a small, but remarkable, granite statue of the little boy surrounded by a group of woodland animals. Sophia and Oliver were deeply touched by this gesture although they took no comfort in it, for the park, and even the statue of the young boy, did little to console them. In fact, it served more as a constant reminder of their heartbreaking loss.

Meanwhile, the little boy continued on his awesome adventure through this very peculiar place with strange humans in their crazy clothing and even stranger structures that they came in and out of. There were also stone walkways that were very uncomfortable beneath his bare feet. The lights around him sparkled in his eyes and the smells of food made his mouth water and his empty stomach do somersaults.

"Where in the world is that amazing smell coming from?" the boy asked himself. So he followed his nose. As he started to get closer and closer to the delicious smell, he could barely contain himself. Finally he located the source of the aroma and burst through the doors of the unique and charming French bakery on Aspen's Main Street. As he did so, the small bell attached to the door jingled with the same excitement the boy felt.

Upon hearing the bell, a plump and rosy-cheeked young woman appeared from behind the display counter wondering what the excessive bell ringing was all about. And what a display cabinet it was to the hungry little boy and his big, bewildered eyes! Hurriedly those eyes darted from the buttery crumb cake, to donuts dripping with icing, to scones bursting with fresh berries, to huge cookies sprinkled in colorful sugar, to the most delicious-looking fruit tarts dripping in chocolate sauce.

"Where in the world do I start?" the boy thought to himself. "This must be a dream. Wait until I tell my family and bring these delicious treats home to them. This adventure will be the best tale in all the land."

The boy gleefully pointed from one sweet treat to another inside of the glass case. The young woman, caught up in his contagious excitement, picked up a big, decorated cookie and handed it over to the little boy in the threadbare clothing. She was charmed by his smile, but alarmed by his ravenous appetite.

And she wasn't the only one in the bakery who was drawn to this fascinating child.

At a small table adjacent to the display counter sat a solemn couple who, a moment earlier, had been conversing quietly over their coffees and croissants. Now they stared with their mouths agape at a sight which was simply beyond their comprehension; this little wonder before them with the familiar smile.

Years from now, when they all reflected back on that day, they still could never explain what made the little boy turn to them at that moment. When he did, a strange feeling of familiarity washed over him. His appetite was forgotten, as he dropped his little hand to his side and his cookie fell to the floor. It was then that the lights from within the pastry case reflected off a sparkling, silver-crested bracelet which hung from the little boy's small wrist.

That's when they knew that their Timmy was finally home.

THE END

AUTHOR BIOGRAPHY

Katie Clarke Head was born and raised in the Suburbs of Philadelphia. She graduated from Fordham University in New York with a BS Degree in Early Childhood Psychology.

Her greatest joy in life is placing a genuine smile on a Child's Face that truly radiates from within and touches their hearts!

She has loved her volunteer work with Special Needs Children and aspires to always encourage every Child to believe in themselves, to know that they are special and unique and to always follow their dreams, no matter what obstacles they may encounter along the way. They truly possess the inner strength to endure ANYTHING and find their "Happily Ever After".

Katie grew up believing in Fairy Tales and through her belief and perseverance, she found her own "Happily Ever After" with her Prince Charming, Charlie, who selflessly invested in this book and in his love for her…I adore and honor you always!, her Cherished Family, who have always embraced her, flaws and all, and have continued to shower her with laughter & love, and to her Beloved Pets, who greet her each and every day with the rare and delightful gift of unconditional love….& of course, lots of "Yucky" licks!!!

*** Stay tuned for the next exciting adventures of The Little Aspen Boy coming soon….You will not believe what happens next…

Printed in the United States
By Bookmasters